WE'RE GOING ON A PICNIC!

WE'RE GOING ON A PICNIC!

Pat Hutchins

RED FOX

ALSO BY PAT HUTCHINS:

Rosie's Walk

Titch

WE'RE GOING ON A PICNIC
A RED FOX BOOK 978 1 782 95022 6

First published in Great Britain by The Bodley Head
an imprint of Random House Children's Publishers UK
A Random House Group Company

First published by Greenwillow Books, New York, 2002
The Bodley Head edition published 2002
Red Fox edition published 2003
This Red Fox edition published 2013

1 3 5 7 9 10 8 6 4 2

Copyright © Pat Hutchins, 2002
The right of Pat Hutchins to be identified as the author of this work has been
asserted in accordance with the Copyright, Designs and Patents Act 1988.

All rights reserved.

Red Fox Books are published by Random House Children's Publishers UK,
61–63 Uxbridge Road, London W5 5SA

www.**randomhousechildrens**.co.uk

www.**randomhouse**.co.uk

Addresses for companies within The Random House Group Limited can be found at: www.randomhouse.co.uk/offices.htm
THE RANDOM HOUSE GROUP Limited Reg. No. 954009
A CIP catalogue record for this book is available from the British Library.

Printed in China

The Random House Group Limited supports the Forest Stewardship Council® (FSC®), the leading
international forest certification organization. Our books carrying the FSC label are printed on FSC®-certified paper.
FSC is the only forest certification scheme endorsed by the leading environmental organizations, including Greenpeace.
Our paper procurement policy can be found at www.randomhouse.co.uk/environment.

For Rachel Isa Baines

"Let's go on a picnic,"
said Hen, Duck, and Goose.
"It's such a lovely day!"

So Hen picked some berries
(because Hen liked berries best),
and Goose picked some apples
(because Goose liked apples best),
and Duck picked some pears
(because Duck liked pears best).
And they put them in the basket.

"We're going on a picnic!" they sang
as they walked across the field.

"This looks like a nice place
for a picnic," said Hen,
and set the basket down.
"I can't wait to eat
some of those berries!"

"It's a bit shady," said Duck.
"Let's go up the hill.
We might find an even nicer place."
"All right," said Hen,
"but it's your turn to carry the basket."

"We're going on a picnic!" they sang
as they walked up the hill.

"This looks like a nice place for a picnic," said Duck, and set the basket down.
"I can't wait to eat some of those pears!"

"It's a bit windy," said Goose.
"Let's go down the hill.
We might find an even nicer place."
"All right," said Duck,
"but it's your turn to carry the basket."

"We're going on a picnic!" they sang
as they walked down the hill.

"This looks like a nice place for a picnic,"
said Goose, and set the basket down.
"I can't wait to eat some of those apples!"

"It's a bit hot," said Hen and Duck.
"Let's go down this path.
We might find an even nicer place."
"All right," said Goose,
"but let's ALL carry the basket."

"We're all going on a picnic!" they sang
as they walked around the lane.

"Oh!" they cried,
and set the basket down.
"We've walked back home,
and we haven't had our picnic!"

"Off we go again," said Hen.
But when they picked up the basket,
it was very light.

And very empty.

"Duck," said Hen, "did you eat the pears?"

"No," said Duck.

"Goose," said Hen, "did you eat the apples?"

"No," said Goose.

"Hen," said Duck and Goose, "did you eat the berries?"

"No," said Hen.

"Then they must have fallen out," said everyone
at the same time.

So Hen picked some more berries
(because Hen liked berries best),
and Goose picked some more apples
(because Goose liked apples best),
and Duck picked some more pears
(because Duck liked pears best).
And they put them in the basket.

"We're going on a picnic!" they sang
as they walked across the field.

"This looks like a nice place for a picnic,"
they all said, and set the basket down.